The Lion Book of
Five-Minute Bedtime Stories

For Sorrel   J.G.

For Mrs Sykes, for a lifetime of encouragement and inspiration x   S.W.

Text copyright © 2009 John Goodwin
Illustrations copyright © 2009 Stephen Waterhouse
This edition copyright © 2009 Lion Hudson

The moral rights of the author and illustrator
have been asserted

A Lion Children's Book
an imprint of
Lion Hudson plc
Wilkinson House, Jordan Hill Road,
Oxford OX2 8DR, England
www.lionhudson.com
UK ISBN 978 0 7459 6143 9
US ISBN 978 0 8254 7944 1

First edition 2009
This printing June 2009
1 3 5 7 9 10 8 6 4 2 0

Typeset in 18/24 Lapidary 333 BT
Printed and bound in China by Printplus Ltd

Distributed by:
UK: Marston Book Services Ltd, PO Box 269, Abingdon, Oxon OX14 4YN
USA: Trafalgar Square Publishing, 814 N Franklin Street, Chicago, IL 60610
USA Christian Market: Kregel Publications, PO Box 2607, Grand Rapids, MI 49501

The Lion Book of
FIVE-MINUTE
Bedtime Stories

Told by John Goodwin

Illustrated by Stephen Waterhouse

LION
CHILDREN'S

Contents

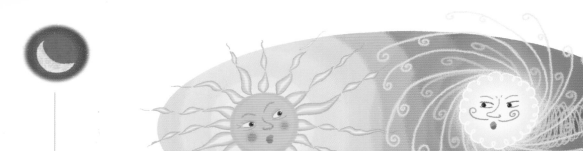

The Wind and the Sun

Gentle persuasion is better than rough force.

HIGH ABOVE THE earth, in the deep blue sky, the wind and the sun were having an argument about who was the stronger of the two.

"You're invisible. No one can ever see you," said the sun. "But everyone knows my sunny face. So how can you say you're stronger than me?"

"Though I'm invisible, people the world over know my power," said the wind. "My soft breezes cool the hottest heads. I can help ships travel the oceans by blowing their sails. Children love me. Without my help, their kites can't take to the skies. The miller can't grind his corn if I don't turn the sails of his windmills, and I help birds glide on my gentle currents."

The sun listened patiently until the wind had run out of puff, and then it said, "I make the sky turn gold at sunset and brilliant blue at noon. With my warmth flowers smile, animals grin, and

humans chortle with joy. What is more powerful in the whole world than the happiness I bring?"

But the wind wasn't listening.

"I do all my work without any black smoke or fire. I don't cause any pollution. I'm a friend of the earth and all those who live on it."

"I take away the ice and cold. Everyone loves to be warm. It makes us all feel so much better," said the sun.

"But I'm more powerful," grumbled the wind.

The sun looked down to the earth and saw a small girl walking through a field with a big scarf wrapped round her neck.

"It's time for a competition," it said. "Whoever can make that child take off her scarf wins."

"Agreed," said the wind. "I'll go first."

The wind filled its cheeks with air and opened its lips just a little. A gentle breeze flowed right down to the girl on earth. She pulled the scarf more closely round her. The wind blew harder and the scarf ends were tossed around. The wind took such a huge intake of breath that its cheeks bulged angrily red. Down came a violent gust which blew the girl right off her feet. The gust turned to gale and the scarf was blown away from the girl's neck high up into the air, but still she hung onto it with the tips of her fingers.

At last, the wind's force was exhausted and the girl once more wrapped the scarf round her neck.

"My turn now," said the sun cheerily as it peeped out round the edge of a cloud so that the child could feel its warmth on her face. Immediately the girl smiled and sat down on a stile in the field. The scarf fell forward a little round her neck. The sun shone more boldly in the sky. Without delay, the child took off her scarf and laid it carefully by her side.

"You've won the competition," cursed the wind angrily.

"So I have," said the sun. "Gentle persuasion is always better than rough force."

Stone Soup

A stranger helps a village share what little they have.

It was a cold, miserable night. The rain lashed down in torrents. A weary traveller with twinkling eyes was seeking shelter. She knocked at many doors in the village but not one was opened to her. The traveller slept as best as she could under the spreading branches of a chestnut tree. Early next morning, she rose shivering with cold.

"Time for a fire," she said as she began to collect scattered bits of wood. As soon as the fire was merrily alight, she took a pan out of her pack and filled it with water from the well. Then she opened her pack again, took out a round stone, and placed it in the middle of the pan.

By this time a few village children had gathered and they peeped out at her from behind the chestnut tree.

"What are you doing?" one of them called.

"I'm making stone soup," replied the traveller.

The children began to giggle. "You can't make soup out of a stone," the biggest of them shouted.

When the water boiled, the traveller tasted the soup.

"Delicious," she said, licking her lips. "But it would be even better with a carrot in it."

The biggest of the children took a long look at the pot of boiling soup and then ran off into one of the village houses.

A few seconds later, the child returned with the biggest carrot the children had ever seen.

"Brilliant," said the traveller, slicing it up and adding it to the pan. After a few more minutes, she sipped the soup again and cried, "Amazing. If only we had an onion."

Another of the children ran off for an onion and more children began to gather by the pan of soup. Just as before, the onion was sliced and added to the soup. The woman tasted the soup again after a few minutes had passed. But this time she shouted, "Magnificent. A turnip would make it perfection."

A turnip was found from one of the houses. Then a beetroot arrived, as did two cabbages, three potatoes, four leeks, and many of the children's parents. Everyone wanted to see what was happening in their usually quiet village. The parents brought even more vegetables as well as cups and bowls with which to have a taste of the soup. All eyes were on the steaming soup now. Lips were licked, bellies rumbled, and hearts rose with the thought of what was to follow.

They were not disappointed. It was the best soup ever, and no matter how many times cups and bowls were filled, the big cooking pot didn't fall empty. The whole village was happily talking and eating the traveller's soup. And later everyone joined in with singing and dancing.

When the traveller left the village, the biggest child scratched her head and said, "Who'd have thought you could really make soup out of a stone?"

The Shoemaker's Slippers

A father learns there's something more important than work.

There was once a poor family who lived in a simple wooden shack. The children, Ruth and Edek, didn't have any toys to play with. Their father was so busy making shoes for all the people in the village that he had very little time for his own family. In fact, his own two children and their mother didn't have shoes to wear. Their feet were always dirty and bruised, and the children couldn't go any further than the shack and its garden.

Because the whole village was poor, their father couldn't charge much for his work and that made him miserable. He laboured for very long hours and the sound of hammering always filled the house.

"Please make shoes for us," pleaded their mother.

"I will," said their father. "Tomorrow I'll make them."

But he was always too tired to complete the task — so the whole family were miserable.

One day, a fine white horse came into the village carrying a very important rider. The shoemaker's children heard a cry echo round the streets.

"The queen is coming, the queen is coming to our village."

The white horse didn't stop at any of the houses until it came to a little wooden shack. Then the queen asked to see the shoemaker. When he saw the queen, he bowed down before her.

"I hear you make fine shoes, shoemaker," she said. "I want you to make me a pair of gold slippers. The finest in the land."

The shoemaker had never made shoes out of gold before but he began the task the next day. He worked without sleeping or eating until he had finished. The slippers were magnificent and gleamed in the sunlight. When the queen saw them, she was delighted. They fitted her dainty feet perfectly.

The shoemaker was given a bag of golden coins for his work. He'd never seen so much money in all his life!

"Now we will be rich and happy," cried Edek and Ruth's mother.

"Now we can have shoes of our own," shouted Ruth.

"Now we can have toys to play with," called Edek.

But the shoemaker was far too exhausted to listen to them and he buried the bag of coins in the back garden. He forbade his family to go anywhere near them and went straight off to bed.

The next day, lots of people hammered on the shack door.

"Make us shoes. The finest in the land," they cried.

It was the same the next day and the next as the shoemaker's fame spread throughout the land. He had never been so busy in all his life — and he couldn't spend any time with his family.

The shoemaker's wife and children were so unhappy that they cried loudly. The shoemaker knew something had to be done urgently. He dug up the bag of coins and walked into the village. When he came home, he closed the doors of the wooden shack.

He put up a big notice in the window saying that he wouldn't
be making any more shoes for a whole week.

He'd invited the whole village to come to a banquet that night
in the back garden. A jester came to tell jokes and the shoemaker's
family laughed together for the first time in years. The very next
day, the shoemaker made his wife and children special shoes.
When they put them on, the whole family wanted to dance.
They danced like they'd never done before in the gleaming,
shiny shoes that he'd made for them with all his love.

The Greatest Pearl
in the World

Sometimes the greatest treasure can be found at home.

THE SEA IS ALIVE with many strange and beautiful creatures. Sea horses bob and ride the currents, dolphins jump right out of the waves and speak their own secret language, while whales blow tiny droplets of water so high into the air that they make their own rainbows.

Tala and Kin dive for another sea creature. For them, the pearl that can be found in the oyster's shell is the only thing that matters. They dream of finding the greatest pearl in the world. It's a gem that's as big as a bird's egg and a thousand times more beautiful. It will shine more brightly than any star, and if they find it they'll be the richest pair in the land.

"Maybe it will be ours today," says Kin as he takes a deep breath and plunges deep into the sea.

"Maybe it will," says Tala as he follows his friend.

But they do not succeed. It's the same the next day and the next and the next. In fact, they have been diving for the great pearl up to now without any luck at all.

Tala is miserable.

"I've had enough of diving every single day," he says, kicking the sand in frustration. "It's time to try a different life."

So he leaves his friend behind him and travels to another country, where he joins a band of entertainers.

"Now I feel free. This is fun," he says.

He works hard at his act by balancing on high stilts but his legs wobble. So he tries to play the bagpipes but the only sound he can make is like an elephant blowing its nose. He tries fire-eating but burns off his beard and melts the bells on his hat.

He persists, however, and after days and days of practice he's ready for his first banquet. It's a wedding in a draughty castle and the entertainers sing, dance, juggle, and tell very funny jokes. Tala does a special act by standing on stilts and blowing the bagpipes at the same time. It all goes well until he tries to do a fancy trick by balancing on one leg with the other high in the air.

Alas, Tala overbalances and falls into the food on the high table. The food goes up in the air and lands with a splat all over the bride's wedding dress.

The wedding guests are outraged and Tala has to leave the entertainers without any money or shelter for the night. He

searches for another job by walking for miles but is unable to find any work. He almost starves and is alone in a strange country. After much unhappiness, he returns to his home with his clothes in rags.

He sees that a grand new house has been built down by the seashore. Its walls are covered in gold and its roof is made of

shining silver, brighter than the stars. Tala walks to the house and sees his old friend Kin inside.

"Kin, it's me, Tala," he says.

"Tala, you look terrible!" cries Kin.

"You look so happy," says Tala.

"Indeed I am," says Kin. "I found a great pearl and sold it for a fortune. We'd have shared it together if you had stayed."

Tala looked at the beauty of the sea and the white waves crashing onto the beach. Their tiny droplets of water made a special rainbow in the sunlight. He was so happy to be home again with his friend. How stupid he'd been to leave.

The Golden Goose

Kindness pays handsome rewards.

THE ELDEST OF three sons set off into the forest to cut wood. There he met a tiny grey-haired old man who said to him, "I see you have brought your lunch with you. Please let me have a taste of your food. I am so hungry."

"I'm not giving you anything, old man. I have work to do," said the boy rudely.

The boy swung his axe and at the very first stroke the head flew off, narrowly missing injuring him. He was scared and ran off home.

A short time later, his younger brother too set out for the forest and met the old man. Just as before, the boy was rude to the grey-haired man.

"Out of my way, you stupid old man," he said. At the first swing of his axe, it got stuck deeply in the trunk of a tree. Despite tugging and pulling and twisting he couldn't free it, and he set off home in a strop.

The youngest son, Raul, who was thought to be a fool by his brothers, set off for the forest and met the tiny grey-haired old man.

When he was asked to share his lunch, he replied, "Of course I will."

After they'd eaten, the old man said, "Since you have such a kind heart, I will give you a gift of good fortune. Cut down the tree over there and you'll find something special."

Raul did as he was told — and when he felled the tree, a goose with golden feathers jumped out. The young boy lifted it up, tucked it under his arm, and set off for an inn where he was going to spend the night.

When Raul was asleep, the innkeeper's three daughters began to make a cunning plan.

"That goose is made of gold," said one daughter, licking her lips.

"Gold will make us rich," said the second, rubbing her hands together.

"We'll sneak into his room and steal it," said the third, taking off her squeaky shoes.

They crept up the stairs of the inn and tiptoed into Raul's room. However, as soon as they touched the goose's feathers, they became stuck to the bird and to each other.

"Help, help" they cried. Raul pretended to be asleep, and they were stuck like glue the whole night through.

The next morning, Raul set off for a grand castle at the top of a hill. He thought he'd find help there in knowing what to do next.

Inside the castle, Raul met a princess who hadn't smiled her whole life. At the sight of the three silly girls entwined in goose feathers and stuck to each other, the princess burst into fits of laughter.

The innkeeper's daughters were freed, and Raul and the princess were soon happily married. They shared a life of giggles together and looked after the golden goose with great care. It repaid them by laying many golden eggs.

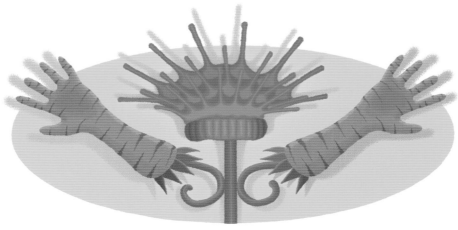

The Emperor's New Clothes

A servant girl proves to be wiser than a silly emperor.

Rosie was a young kitchen servant at the emperor's palace. The emperor loved one thing more than anything in his whole life – and that was clothes. They were made out of silks from Persia, satins from Arabia, feathers from the Orient, and wool from Iceland, all made up in astonishing and rather eccentric styles. The clothes shone and shimmered and dazzled in the sunlight. The whole city turned out to see the emperor's amazing clothes when he paraded through the streets.

After a while, the emperor became bored with his clothes. One day, two new tailors arrived at the palace to design different ones for him. Rosie saw them arrive and took an immediate dislike to them. She peeped through a tiny crack in the kitchen door and saw and heard how smarmy they were.

"We'll make you clothes finer than you have ever seen before," they promised the emperor. "They will look like clothes that

nobody else has ever worn before. They will be so special that your heart will melt just to think about them."

The emperor gazed at them both with his mouth wide open. Rosie saw one of the tailors wink at the other as if they were playing a game.

"They're tricksters, not real tailors at all," thought Rosie.

But the emperor was blind to the wink and the trick. He asked, "What will the clothes look like?"

"Stunning," came the tailors' answer. "Truly magnificent."

"Stunning," repeated the emperor with a huge smile on his face. "Truly magnificent," he drooled, picturing himself in total, wonderful splendour.

"Oh yes," said the tailors. "And only very clever people will be able to see them. Isn't that wonderful?"

"Indeed," said the emperor, so lost in admiration for himself that he wasn't listening to what they were saying.

The two tailors moved into the palace. They told everyone that they were working very hard indeed but Rosie didn't believe them. Every time she saw them, they were either playing silly games or gazing out of the window. Rosie wanted so much to tell the emperor that the new tailors were a big mistake but she knew he wouldn't listen to a humble servant girl.

At last, everything was ready for the emperor's new clothes to be shown in public. The whole city had talked about nothing else for weeks. Rosie had been dreading what would happen and had hidden herself away in the kitchen for days.

The tailors helped the emperor into magnificent clothes that only the clever could see. When the clock struck midday, the palace gates were thrown wide open. Everyone in the huge crowd that had gathered strained their necks to take a good look at the emperor. After all, this was going to be his finest moment.

At last, the emperor appeared on the palace steps. There was a hush in the crowd followed by a gasp and then a giggle.

Everybody was laughing at the emperor. Instead of jewelled finery, he was wearing his shabby old pants and darned vest. The tailors had made him no clothes at all.

It was a moment Rosie had prepared for. She ran down the palace steps carrying a bundle. Before anyone could stop her, she slipped some clothes neatly over the emperor's head. Then she sprang back. Everyone could see she'd made a giant plum-coloured robe that covered the emperor from head to foot.

The crowd cheered loudly. Rosie had saved the day.

The Three Bundles of Sticks

Families are stronger when they work together.

A POOR WIDOW HAD three children to look after all by herself in a little crooked house. The children argued all day, every day. Seth, the eldest boy, was lazy and wouldn't help his mother.

One day, his sister Ellen decided to play a trick on Seth. She hid his only pair of trousers where he couldn't find them.

"What did you do that for?" he said to her.

"It's just a joke," she said.

"Well, it's not funny," he cried.

"I think it is," said Ellen, laughing loudly.

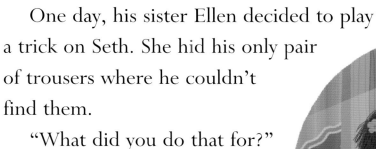

All day they argued. James, the youngest of the three, became angry too and played his drums as loud as he could to drown out their row. Their poor mother found the house so noisy that she went down to her tiny flower garden. There she found quietness amongst the sweet-smelling, brightly coloured plants.

As the children grew older, they argued more and more. Ellen liked to bring her friends round to the house to play games. Seth and James argued because of the drums, and the two of them argued with Ellen because the house was always crowded with her friends. Ellen didn't like boys at all, especially her brothers because they were stupid, rude, and never washed.

Their mother was at her wit's end with all three of them.
One day, she pulled them out into the front of the garden,
where she'd laid three bundles of sticks.

"See if you can break these," she said.

"Too easy," said James.

"Too boring," said Ellen.

"Too much like hard work," said Seth.

But their mother was determined, and at last they gave in and
set to work. James pulled and strained. Ellen tugged. Seth yawned
and sighed and eventually heaved and wrenched. No matter how
hard they tried, not one of them could break the bundles.

Their mother untied the sticks so that they fell separately
at their feet.

"Now see if you can break them," she said.

James snapped them all in half immediately. So did Ellen. Seth took a little longer. Then their mother gave them all a long hard look.

"Our family is like those sticks," she said. "If we all work together as one, we'll be strong. No one will be able to break us. But if we continue to argue, we're divided as a family and we'll be broken for sure."

The children stood ashamed as their mother went down to her tiny flower garden. James looked at Seth and Ellen but nobody spoke. Ellen was the first to break the silence.

"Time for action," she said.

That evening, the three of them cleaned the house, which they'd never done before. There was not one word of argument between them. They cooked the dinner, too. Their mother picked the flowers to put on the table.

The Giant's Footprint

A young girl finds her courage in a difficult time.

ALL THE VILLAGE people stared down. Below them was a huge footprint. Everyone was silent. At last someone said, "What made it?"

One of the village elders sighed and said, "Only one creature can make a snow footprint this big. It's a giant."

The word "giant" echoed round the frightened people.

"It must have come out from the mountains," said another elder.

"We'll have to take shelter in the cave tonight," said a third elder, "in case the giant comes back again."

They lit a fire in the entrance of the cave, huddled close, told stories, and tried to keep cheerful. It was past midnight before everyone had settled into a fitful sleep.

However, one small girl was still wide awake. Martha peeped out of the mouth of the cave with her eyes fixed towards the

mountains high in the sky. Was this where the giant lived?
What sort of creature was he? Why was everyone afraid of him?

Something moved in the darkness. The moon came out from
behind a cloud and Martha could suddenly see very clearly. High
above her head was the face of the giant. It was not scary at all.
What was he doing there? The giant looked sad and far more
frightened than she'd ever imagined. She could see his body was

as thin as an icicle and that he must be very hungry indeed. After a few seconds, he turned towards the mountains and disappeared into them.

The next morning, people were still afraid. Some wanted to leave the village, never to return, but the snow was too deep for them to travel. Martha knew it was time to speak.

"He's really not scary at all," she said. "He's not going to hurt us."

"You know nothing, little girl," said one of the elders. "Leave this to us grown-ups."

"I saw him and looked into his eyes," said Martha. "They were so sad. He must be very hungry as there's no food for him in the mountains in the winter."

"You were dreaming," said the elder with a rough laugh.

"I did see him," said Martha. "He needs our help. We must find food for him and leave it outside the cave."

"What nonsense," said the elder.

But Martha stood her ground. "If you'd seen him, you'd know I'm telling the truth."

The villagers argued long and hard about what Martha had said, and opinions were divided. At last, a vote was held and most were in favour of her plan. That night in the cave many people peeped out towards the food, and shortly after midnight the giant appeared.

The giant and the villagers became more and more friendly.

They saw him every day as he collected the food they left out for him during the harsh winter. It wasn't easy at first, as some of the villagers were still very suspicious and the giant was scared of seeing so many people. But soon the bravest of the people let the giant lift them up gently and take them to his magnificent mountain home for a while. You can be sure that Martha was the first to visit.

Green Leaves

A land is made to live again when acorns are planted.

A SAD WOMAN WHO was all alone in the world set off to find a new life for herself. She travelled to a bare land where almost nothing grew and very few people lived. She passed empty tumbledown houses and a few twisted trees. The woman bought some sheep and a dog and became a shepherd. She moved into one of the empty houses and lived a simple life.

As the days passed, she collected acorns from the trees. She planted them every morning and afternoon, and soon their green shoots appeared out of the ground. She watched over them like they were her own children – and she even spoke to them.

"Grow, trees, grow," she'd say. "Lift up your tender heads and look at the world. Rejoice in the summer sun. Drink up the raindrops. Don't let the wind and cold weaken your hearts, for you must grow fine and strong. Grow, my children, grow."

And so the trees grew.

A few were nibbled by animals.

One or two were blown away in the storms.

One lost all its leaves to the pecks of birds.

But most prospered and grew tall.

As they did, the woman changed too.

Her body became tanned by the sun.

Her face grew round and jolly.

Her heart was content.

The woman had to travel further and further to plant the acorns, but she didn't miss a single day. She had to rise early in the mornings and it was late at night before she returned home.

But she didn't complain, for the green carpet grew and grew until it covered many miles.

Years passed and the huge acorn forest prospered, just as the woman knew it would. The roots of the trees held water where once it had drained away on the barren land. Small pools of water formed and then streams and rivers. Animals came to the forest. Squirrels danced along the branches of the trees. Deer, pigs, and goats grazed on the lush grass that grew by the pools. Fish swam in the streams and rivers. Families returned to live in the empty houses and rebuilt them as happy homes.

Children played freely, and everywhere there was abundance in the days of contentment.

Maybe the people forgot about the old woman who'd started it all, for it was way in the past. People's memories are short sometimes. But the trees remembered. Oak woodlands are ancient and hearts of oak never forget. The trees were strong and tall, proud in the knowledge that they'd made the woman so happy.

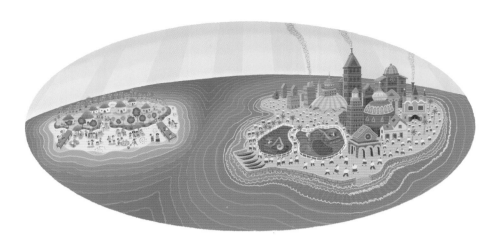

Two Islands

Greed does not succeed.

IN THE MIDDLE of the ocean there are two islands, one larger than the other. People on the small island enjoy life. It's fun all day every day for them. They enjoy lounging on the beach in the warm sun. They have no leader and everyone is equal. Their island uses no money. There are enough fish in the sea and plenty of berries and fruits on the trees for them to eat. Some days they fly kites decorated with paints made out of plants that grow along the seashore, and make patterns from beautiful pebbles on the beach.

On the big island, everything is very different. Here the people are always busy, working from dawn until dusk. They use blue shells for money and build fancy houses. The big island has a leader who is very powerful.

One day, the small islanders heard a relentless grating noise coming from the big island.

"What's that?" they asked.

"What ever it is, it's horrible," they agreed.

They peered into the far distance but they couldn't see what was happening. The noise continued for weeks, as did their headaches, and they couldn't sleep at all as the sounds could be heard 24 hours a day.

With the noise still around, a fleet of canoes came to visit the small island. Big islanders jumped out of them and began lifting all the pebbles into the canoes. The small islanders ignored this at first but when it was repeated day after day, they tried to protest.

"Hello. What are you doing?" they called — but the big islanders took no notice.

"Please leave the pebbles alone," they cried, but still the big islanders continued to load them into their canoes and sail away with them. When there were no pebbles left on the beach, the small islanders decided to send a group to the big islands to find out why the pebbles were being stolen.

As soon as they landed on the big island, they were captured and taken to a building site. There they saw a giant palace was being built close to the sea that grew so high, it blotted out the sun. It was made out of red bricks, the clay of which was being dug out of deep pits along the seashore by huge and very noisy diggers. The walls of the building were decorated with the beautiful pebbles from the small island beach. The prisoners were told that the palace was to be the leader's new home.

"Get the small islanders to work immediately," shouted the leader. "They've not come here to be idle."

Weeks passed and the small islanders worked like slaves to make the palace bigger and bigger as the clay pits became deeper and deeper.

One stormy day when the winds howled and the waves were as big as mountains, the pits flooded.

The palace walls creaked and groaned as the waves pounded the shore. Cracks appeared like giant hands all over the building and finally it collapsed into the sea — and what was left of the big island disappeared under the waves.

A big rescue began and everyone headed off to the small island, where they all live happily to this day. The big islanders saw how much better life was on the small island, and they soon joined in with flying their kites and taking it easy on the sunny beach.